PREFACE

Childhood - bedtime stories from a man lying next to me, staring at the ceiling, moving his hands to describe each scene, his voice warm and transporting me to snow covered mountains, 12000 feet above sea level with mere words.

Anecdote 1

"The skies were clear that day, I woke up almost 30 minutes before the alarm went off. Our regional ADG (a title that I remember to this day) along with high ranking officers were visiting our site. I took an early bath with mildly heated water, oiled my legs, wore 2 pairs of woolen socks, shaved and got dressed.

Our meeting point was near the pass where the dynamite blasts would happen high above, and my job as the site engineer was to brief about progress and issues at the site. About 3 minutes into the conversation with one of the inspecting officers – the man was half a foot taller than me, broad, with a thick moustache - we heard the blasts.

At this point, he leaned over to look at a stretch of road below and I moved to my left and almost organically, we exchanged places. I was standing exactly where he was a while ago, and he was where I stood.

And I was explaining something to him about our strategy to build and stopped mid-sentence. A single boulder, no bigger than the size of a human skull fell on his head, probably dislodged due to the blasts above.

Thud! And the officer collapsed to the ground, his head smashed.

Till that day I did not believe in supernatural, higher powers. If we didn't trade places that moment, I wouldn't be here telling you this story..or maybe I would.."

I must have been 10 when my dad told me this story. He also spoke of how he and his team of engineers helped with funerals for colleagues killed in dynamite blasts, or during road construction high up in the mountains – sometimes, these were sky burials.

The BRO (Border Roads Organization) undertakes projects in India and friendly countries. These projects typically include developing roads, bridges, and airfields in hostile environments shunned by private enterprises, whether due to security concerns related to hostilities, or because of environmental challenges.

Anecdote 2

"I was in Andaman and Nicobar those days. Each evening, after the evening *chai* and snacks, I used to get out of my tent, walk into the forest, meet my colleagues in other tents, some of them a mile away and tread back to my tent before dinner.

That day was no exception. I came out of my tent, it was getting dark and so I went back in and got my torch. A red and white Ever Ready with a big white switch.

"Sir, going for your walk?" One of the many draftsmen and engineers drinking outside asked.

"Yes.." I nodded and walked past the flag post denoting our tent, out into the forest. Darkness fell all around quite suddenly, and I was looking for the trail that I usually walk on.

Suddenly I heard a 'hiss' close to my feet, froze and next thing I know, I was looking into the eyes of a Cobra, half standing, almost at my waist level, at striking distance. And at the very same moment, on instinct, I switched on the torchlight. Right on its eyes. It was so still, almost acknowledging my fear.

"Sir! Keep the torch shining on its eyes, and slowly walk backwards. Slowly.." I barely heard the sharp, whispering advice from the men behind. My entire being's focus was on this almost-on-its-tail-creature, so ready to strike!

All of these must have happened in a few seconds. In my mind, slow was not an option. I remember following its head, seeing it sway just a little to the right. I switched off the torchlight and simultaneously ran left with all the speed I could muster, away from

BOR DER LESS

INDRAJEET DASGUPTA

First Published in July 2019

ISBN: 978-93-5347-612-0

BLUE ROSE PUBLISHERS
www.bluerosepublishers.com
info@bluerosepublishers.com
+91 8882 898 898

Cover Design:
Mark Hernandez
Mohd Arif

Typographic Design:
Tanya Raj Upadhyay

Editor:
Apoorva Khare

Distributed by: Blue Rose, Amazon, Flipkart, Shopclues

a possible strike. The men were already up with torchlights shining all over the thick forest.

"Bach gaye Sirji" (You got saved Sir)

Both stories are anecdotes from one man. A man with unshakeable integrity, rare character and what I call military precision, he was never late for anything – my Dad.

Borderless is dedicated to him – he who built fearless roads high in the Himalayas, risking his very life; tunnels, culverts and bridges in the faraway Andamans, majestic high rises and mini-cities in the East of India. A man who has been described by family and friends as someone who was always at work. Either mending something in the house, or preparing for a card party at home later (thanks to my mom's legendary hosting skills) or simply cooking sambhar (a lentil based vegetable stew), he was always on the go, till the last day..

Mr. Swapan Kumar Dasgupta – my real-life hero, my father – this is for you.

I have always believed in a borderless world.

Human greed for more - land, resources, water led to colonization in the past and in many cases, the colonizers created the modern-day borders. In pre-modern world, anything away from the capital was considered 'borderland.' Most countries today have some form of border control to limit the movement of people, animals and goods in and out of those countries.

Thankfully, music, fine arts, sculpture, dance forms, books are all borderless. I have seen strangers exchanging music lists at airports, I have spoken to 'exchange' students talking about how well they fit into a new culture and I have listened to senior citizens talk about how easy it is now to connect with anyone, anywhere – something they were never able to do in 40-50 years of their lives.

Technology will continue to play a pivotal role in this century to bring humanity together, at all levels. If you search "farthest places on earth," you would find two cities – Rosario in Argentina and Xinghua in China, separated by 19,996 kms. And we know how long it would take for the residents of both cities to see each other on social media – blink!

Borderless is about modern philosophies borne out of the new realities of this century, it attempts to chronicle events, capture moments and conversations and critiques the norm. I hope you, my reader, connect to many of these at a personal level – that would be my ultimate fulfilment.

This book wouldn't have been made possible without a long list of selfless souls who have egged me on at various times to just do one thing – *write*.

Mrs. Swapna Dasgupta, my mother, whose innumerable messages in the past months, with one central theme – "Blessings for the book," overrode all other sundry questions or concerns about my wellbeing. Thanks Ma.

Thanks also to my closest buddies - Keshuv Tandon and Bharat Gopalakrishnan for egging me on. My sincerest thanks to Resil Fuscablo for going out of her way for marketing the book in The Philippines, Mark Hernandez for creating my book videos, 'Zy' for the book images, Mr. Jimmy Belleza for allowing me on his Happiness Guru show and to my dear sister Shubhra Dasgupta for believing that the book would 'happen' one day. And thanks also to my extended Facebook family for their good wishes.

I want to thank the entire team at Blue Rose, my publishers, for being patient with a 'working author.' Ria, Arpit, Aadhaar, Tanya and the ever innovative and industrious Mr. Syed – thank you! You have been a fantastic team for a new author. Greatly respect your suggestions, ideas and edits. All the very best to you.

I present this book to that one soul that matters the most – my daughter, the wise one – Avantika Dasgupta

CONTENTS

1. **Millennium - A Bevy of Poems** 2
   - 31st 2
   - Afghan War and The Big O 4
   - Damn Sad 6
   - Mark the Great 8
   - London Hit 10
   - My Phone...12
   - The Brothers 14
   - City of Dreams Besieged.......................................16
   - The Real O...18
   - Was it the Spring? 20
   - Wild West Miracle 22
   - Geronimo 24
   - 7 Years On… 26
   - Red Planet Selfie and The Greatest Show 28
   - Death of Humanity 30
   - Marathon Mourning...32
   - The Voice of Peace..34
   - Alexandrian Fall..36
   - Same 38
   - Queen and the City of Arts....................................40
   - Egress...42
   - 21st Century Duck...44
2. Smart Mornings...46
3. Recipe Emotionnel 48
4. Discipline 52
5. Spirit of a Man 54
6. Art and Commerce..56
7. Unsocial Media 60
8. Chapter Eight 64

9. 21st Century Duck 68
10. Values 72
11. Kings of Laze 74
12. Diverse 76
13. Ode to a Leader 78
14. Right Hand 80
15. Goalless 82
16. Artiste 86
17. CEO 88
18. Protector 90
19. Ancient Land and The King of Promises 92
20. The Three Drivers 96
21. On Divorce and Separation 98
22. The Boss 102
23. Material 104
24. Terminal 108
25. Heads of States 110
26. Opinionated 112
27. Listen 116
28. Déjà vu – 118
29. Tarot 122
30. Ambition 124
31. Odds 126
32. Sheep 130
33. Return of the Son 134
34. Of Godmen and Spirituality 138
35. Neo-Colonist 142
36. Humanity Born 144
37. Anger 148
38. Crested Ibis 150
39. Guinness 152
40. Family 154
41. Crawlers and The Blue Horizon 156

42. Limitless Ltd. 160

43. Beautiful Planet 162

44. Power 166

45. Romantique 168

46. Poison Ivy 172

47. Death of an Act 174

48. Long Faces 178

49. Interview Incarnate 182

50. The Fearless Badger 186

51. Late Grammy 188

52. Music Forgotten 190

53. Corporate Noose 194

54. Older... 196

55. Blue Moon 200

56. Dating in the Dark 202

57. Monk in The City 206

58. Juice 208

59. Mountain Shoes.. 210

60. The Professionals on Politics.. 214

61. Airmos 218

62. Digital 220

63. From Him to Her.. 222

64. The Revenge at Bali 224

65. Creatures of The Possible 228

66. Of Things to come 230

MILLENNIUM - A BEVY OF POEMS

31ˢᵀ

The Harbour, The Eye, The Tower, The Clock,

All came alive as the skies lit up,

Every eyeball worth its salt, marveled and took stock!

Oh what a spectacle it was, humanity welcomed a fresh new hundred...

Years of hope, prosperity, potential and souls kindred!

AFGHAN WAR AND THE BIG O

Two decades before this display, when the guerrillas and armies clashed,
A tall young rich lad, boy was he sad, put his money down and smashed.
Humanity like never before or ever after, oh they called him pure evil,
In hindsight, he and his actions were pre-ordained, far from civil.

Cooking up an impossible dream for a frenzied clan baying for a certain blood,
He created an army to lift the word of their God, used hatred and prejudice to flood…
Hearts and minds so much so, they got sold on this man's intent so low,
Four crafts altered Humanity's very core from trust and love to quid pro quo.

DAMN SAD

Meanwhile the super and the power conspired and overthrew,
A man and his government, dug him out, court-tried and slew,
Just so humanity's oil and fuel so corrupt,
Flows on uninterrupted, lest their currency disrupt.

MARK THE GREAT

Amidst all the missiles, hatred and battle smoke,
Emerged this young and ever smiling bloke..
Rating the ladies hot or not, got him into sweet trouble
a lot!
Tugging on the hierarchy – of love, belonging and
esteem,
He made this world open up an ocean of pent-up
steam.

LONDON HIT

And then it happened once more, right under the
Queen's nose,
Men, women going to work, another Thursday is what
they suppose.
Three underground and one bomb atop, hits Greatness
as much, so please stop!
Forsaking everything for what they believe, four young
souls made 52 pop.

MY PHONE

Technology follows terror it seems, cause the guru
offers an apple so dear,
Revolution in your palm! Music, the smarts, and the
voices calm,
A phone so proud, that the masters are now slaves,
And billions get sucked into the new i – Oh My, Oh
My!

THE BROTHERS

Just about this time so high, the world's monies were drawing nigh,
The brothers went first, then like dominoes the markets crash and cry!
Too many were not paying the banks for the home that wasn't,
The aftershocks of a depression so deep, we vowed never again. Mustn't!

CITY OF DREAMS BESIEGED

And then the ancient land's business hub, besieged by the Satan's club,
Twelve spots of humanity waiting, caring, lounging – to smithereens get blown,
Welcome to the Devil's own, a city halts while the world stops and watches,
A neighbor's design to awe, burn and roast, turns around, the news lens latches.

THE REAL O

Guess what happens right after? Yes, guessed right,
Prince Charming enter!
The audacity of hope embodied in his lanky frame, a
new leader at the center.
He brought change, decency and a certain character to
the greatest chair ever,
One that tried, upheld values and had humanity at the
core, yet clever.

WAS IT THE SPRING?

Single man selling his wares, on a mildly cold
December morn,
Stopped and harassed by a policewoman, his dignity
shorn.
Set self and desert nations on fire, a social media
revolution with fallouts dire,
Governments toppled, homeless millions, was this what
they foresaw, Sire?

They called it the Spring, we know it doesn't ring.

WILD WEST MIRACLE

Another desert tragedy followed with miners trapped
so deep,
Families, governments, and the world pray and weep.
A message breaks their bated breaths, all 33 safe and
sound!
Buried alive and miraculously saved, human hope and
faith abound.

GERONIMO

The tall, young, rich lad is now old of hiding in caves,
safe houses and such,
While they hunt him down, he and his wives in cozy
comfort but trudge,
And then, one night of hellish swoop, whirring birds
with armed troops,
Annihilate the old boy, his beliefs and endless verbal
loops.

7 YEARS ON...

Meanwhile, the seven-year war intensifies, half a
million perished,
Refugees cornered, facing icy death, far from their
dreams cherished.
A civil war to thwart those in power has always been a
case,
Of humanity seeking its primary rights – freedom and
a little grace.

RED PLANET SELFIE AND
THE GREATEST SHOW

Technology, once more, breaks the streak of terror,
strife and gore,
A roving eye, takes a selfie on a red planet shore.
Meanwhile, the Bond amongst men sure meets the
Queen,
The greatest sporting show on earth must now begin!

DEATH OF HUMANITY

"The greatest glory in living, lies not in never failing, but in rising,
Every time we fail!" He who said those words is no more, we still realising,
A leader who reminded humanity of its truest self, the power of hope,
And to see all men as equal, an icon of justice… what a loss to cope!

MARATHON MOURNING

Yes, terror comes back – with two bangs so grim,
Runners maimed near the finish line, sans many a
limb.
Bodies tired, overheated and dehydrated – they are but
stunned,
Blood, water bottles, flesh and coke, yet again a
religion shunned.
For waylaid youth, with designs uncouth.

THE VOICE OF PEACE

Peace after terror, "Thank you, my father, for not
clipping my wings
And letting me fly." Hit in the head by a bullet, a teen
activist springs,
A second life granted for greatness, the warrior woman
speaks of rights,
Blogs against bans, reopens schools, finally her voice
wafts to Nobel heights.

ALEXANDRIAN FALL

And then the Great Greeks fall, failing to repay,
Like in life, so for nations – be frugal if you may.
Be indebted to Him, not to funds and banks,
Eight years for the cradle of the West to revive its
ranks.

SAME

Politics and religion have their Digitus Medius in the
union of genders,
Same gender against the law, Nature and Him. Oh,
such mind benders!
Humanity says same souls first, then your gender, color
and creed,
Finally it's legal, they say "Aye!" A whole new happy
breed!

QUEEN AND THE CITY OF ARTS

Meanwhile, the Queen records the longest ever reign,
At eighty-nine years and some, she redefines style and
refrain.
Next, the city of Arts goes under the siege, revenge for
airstrikes it seems,
Kids of the New World Order cutting short ordinary
lives and dreams.

EGRESS

And then the will of the Great Ones divided, they
debate to stay or leave,
Play host to strangers and risk your wallet? Their pride
makes chests heave!
The debates continue and the pubs come alive,
The moment of decision is here, Mr. Civil it's for you
to survive.

21ST CENTURY DUCK

The Days of The Duck have now begun, the ugly campaign over,
He grins and bares, waves and jeers, roasts and jokes on whatsoever,
A constructor, a celebrity, and now, the leader of the free,
Does The Duck ever think of conscience, morality and legacy?

SMART MORNINGS

There exists a global culture and oneness. From Angola to Yemen, from the Falkland Islands right up to Calgary, and from the South Atlantic to the Barents Sea, humanity wakes up like a programmed Android app. There is a live generation that still remembers their dads after waking up, stretching in bed, throwing a beatific smile at them, and them beaming right back. Now, there are two smartphones between the son and the father, same time in the mornings.

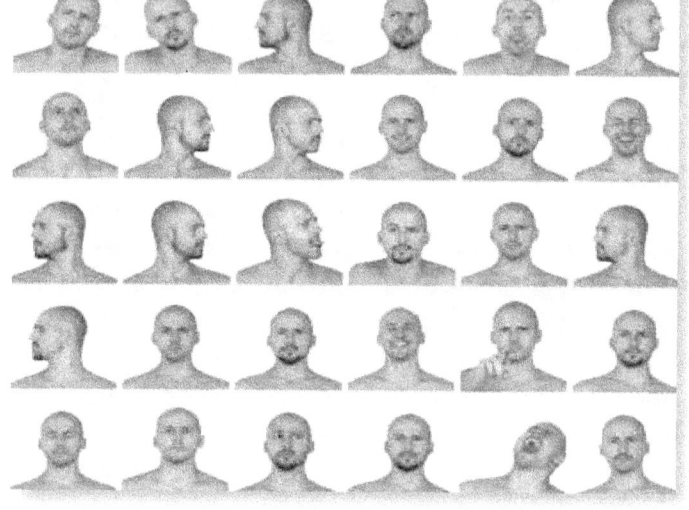

RECIPE EMOTIONNEL

Early morning love and lust, the fond smell of home,
Ruffled sheets, hair and wear, the plunge in scented
foam.
Cheery breakfast, joyous laughs and kisses for the day,
On your way to work or war, not a nerve did fray.

Your mind is joyful, full of zest, and then it hits you
bare,
The worldly noise, traffic and voice, and fetid urban
air.
The first flushes of pinkish anger wafting through your
mind,
"This hanging wire right above, are these guys so
blind?!"

The office elevators warrant morning smiles, you talk to
many more,
By the time you reach your desk, it's work and work
galore!
Through the day they sneak in and out, all the
emotions here,
Regret, guilt, hate, contempt, shock, and pure fear.

That then is your average day of what they call work,
On your way back, your joyous feet test the engine
torque.
The wife seems happy, joyful kids rush to meet and
hug,
Paradise found! Is what you say at the gentle, hearty
tug.

At dinner, it's tender talk, contentment and pleasure,
All the world can take a break, this bliss the real
treasure!
A lively meal, wife's sweet desserts and a dash of
jealousy,
The neighbor's lawn has a snowball bush, did you
even see?

DISCIPLINE

Her little heart has captured the essence of daddy's sermon at yesterday's dinner.

"Tomorrow is your first day at school."

While she pretends to sleep, trying hard to keep the rhythm of her breath constant, her heart is drumming away.

The yellow bus will halt right outside her front porch and she will be half-lifted by dad and half-collected by the bus man. Mom said hers is the third pickup. She will say hello to two of her newest friends and settle into the first window seat on the left. She could see the shadow of her flying hair and the roundness of her cheeks on the empty seat beside her. The excitement of her first day at school makes her smile, and almost right then, mom pulls her towards herself in a warm embrace. Her last discipline-less night.

SPIRIT OF A MAN

For what's a man whose heart has not been seared nor
singed,
For him, whose burning eyes never wore glasses tinged.
Fallen and judged, rising each time, toothpaste hits the
brush,
For all the storms couldn't make his mighty spirit crush.

With each fall, he sees himself in the mirror to say,
I did it the way I knew, ain't there a single hopeful ray?
The honest mirror thinks, then smiles,
Your spirit, my man, will take you through all the sun-
kissed miles.

Till you reach where you belong,
Even though it took you so long.

ART AND COMMERCE

At this busy, wintry, northern country Airport, Art has chosen to sit on the aisle seat next to the recliners facing the runways. While taking in the symmetry of the white arches above, he is reminded of a pristine church. Just around this time, Commerce steps off the travellator. He shuffles around 3-4 rows of seats, rejects a few empty ones with his hawkish, thick-brow eyes, crosses over multiple passenger feet and plonks onto the seat next to Art. He places his leather duffel between his legs and a smaller case on his lap, and with practiced ease, straightens up the newspaper with a series of crisp papery sounds.

Careful not to ignore this change in his private orb, Art gently shifts left, crossing his right leg over his left, looking out at the vast emptiness of the runway. His chiseled jaw tilts away from the perilously close left edge of Commerce's newspaper. The colorful news in the middle of the paper makes Art look back sharply – it's a full center spread of the pageant beauties.

"Watched it?" Art asks in his half-deep baritone.

"Nah, never found the time." The abruptness in Commerce's voice makes the sensitive Art stop dead in his tracks.

"You?" Commerce didn't bother to look up from the paper while asking the question.

"Was right there in the front!"

The laughter that came out of the sharp-suited Commerce was akin to that of a septuagenarian, low and raspy.

His body shook, but the eyes didn't convey happiness. Amused, Art asked "So, you don't like pageants...?" Folding the paper, Commerce replied, "Was the chief sponsor, unfortunately had meetings to attend in the same hotel. So, you flew in just for this?"

Smiling, Art locks his smoky grey eyes on Commerce's, "Yes, I dressed them – all of them."

UNSOCIAL MEDIA

Local gossip gone global, is all that social media is,
All your likes validate me, for all the trust I miss.
Suddenly, the world shows love and fresh new friends each day,
Share each of your private acts, ones mom wouldn't dare say.

I am brushing, I am jogging, am having breakfast now,
How long do you think they shall 'like' before they all take the vow?
Of not watching inane posts and other people's lives,
And focus on what's important, themselves and their wives!

Sharing milestones is another thing, but to lay a life so bare?
Your life is yours alone, save those moments to share,
With granddaughters and their friends many years hence,

When you talk, and they huddle close sans any pictures thence.

For the power of human stories have endured the dawn of time,
For machines write poems too, but with human hearts don't chime.

CHAPTER EIGHT.

CHAPTER EIGHT

One day I shall be gone too soon, so you survive, thrive,
This world will push, love and strip you, while you work a week of five,
You shall suffer the gift of the unknown, the guilt of knowledge,
For each meaningful success, you shall pay a defined wage.

Kicked in the gut, butt and nut,
You finally grow wise, or into a naive mutt,
You project your life and times on a screen, marry or keen,
Wave the kids byes at airports, just to get back to that meeting.

And thence one day, the soul shall preside,
With the mind and heart in deep obeisance,
"The greater good," the soul shall say, "will determine your lousy stay."
The mind says, "Objection, what use is the greater good?
Without shelter, respect and some good food?
And without the mention on chapter eight?"

"Here lies a great man, who was the perfect kid, student, husband and father,
Oh, also a friend, coach and benefactor.
Those seven selfless roles I say, must make way for the eighth chapter."

Cause the eighth is selfish, ruthless, blasé with instinct primal,
One that manipulates, schemes, takes it all,
So when you turn the pages of them 'Successes',
Your name is enshrined, chapter eight, at the top, no less.

It's the heart's turn indeed, it smiles at both, soul and mind, and speaks,
"Interesting, you said it all my friends – my prayer is for just a few weeks,
Of love, gratefulness and silent prayers for the man next to us,
He may be in his chapter eight, but our hearts should win him over thus."

21ST CENTURY DUCK

This duck is a reluctant amphibian,
Business his land, his realpolitik at sea,
Reviled, abused, denounced… this man,
For decades four, the great lakes' goose and gander
Quacked his name, their leader to be!

Now when the duck really leads, on his solo flight,
They wanna shoot him down? Oh what a sight!
Duck and his raft, made big changes on the Great
Lakes' Net,
New ducks need to pay more for the fast lane, and not
fret!
His chosen white ducks now judge the commune,
They lift the ban on dump and waste, the Lakes no
more immune.

Last and not the least, the white ducks let the hunters roam free,
With guns in hand and no control, they wade the waters with deadpan glee.
250 years in the making, the Great Lakes are now but shaking,
With the fury of the Duck's misdirection, waiting, wailing, faking.

Will they peck so hard on his golden plume,
And all his duck-man failings exhume?
Or will they remember it was them who fed,
Greed and greed alone made the duck so dead.

VALUES

Dads are clients, moms the HR, and everyone else the employees. Moms teach you values at a young age – respect people, make friends, thereby increasing your network, don't think bad/evil about anyone, when you grow up, do good for the community, and finally focus on your dad (client) – keep him on your side!

Dads, on the other hand, talk from experience and they go, "Spend wisely (profitability), be careful with what you say about other people (confidentiality), you can actually make money being honest (integrity), and lastly, always find a better way to do things (innovate)." Corporate values are values that you and I always knew and lived, it's just that they are now on digital screens.

KINGS OF LAZE

Some of them keep the ashtrays on the mound around their navels, gentle cushions of adipose tissue sloping down from the base of their male nipples, plateauing out, before sloping down to the nether. Their legs are almost always stretched out on a smaller piece of furniture kept away from the lounge recliner while they smoke, watch, and drink.

They also possess this rare ability to find corners, for space, safety and security. In cinemas, aircrafts, restaurants – you will see them in the corners. Safe because they can amble out easily during emergencies, secure since the corners provide that sense of comfort and space since one leg is always spread out indecently. When they need food, they transform – snapping their fingers even while the steward is looking right into their eyes – and make all sorts of noise if there is a delay.

They are the urban kings of laze.

DIVERSE

For a brief moment, imagine yourself as God as you know Him to be, and you look at your vast creation from way above, and then, under your breath, murmur—

"You named it the knowledge age. Knowledge to unify or separate, to prosper or flounder, to laugh or sulk? My children shake off this uniformity in language, habits, ideas of success and inane pursuits. Rise, awake, and as they say, take one step back. And thou shalt see the lie. Be diverse, be individuals – that was the idea."

ODE TO A LEADER

For a cool one like you, boss or client,
Are but words not pliant.
Your zeal all evident, each moment if we may,
A purpose so great, with nary a nay.

We shall be continuous, indeed and in quest,
Of making 'better' our newest best,
Since better has hope, that best doesn't...

Thank You,
Your Team

RIGHT HAND

The actor is at it again. He has been playing this game for an eternity. The right hand is a maestro in motion, a fine example of singularity of purpose, an uncanny intelligence guides its grace and fluidity in public. Never can you flinch, make an awkward movement – that's the master's voice. And so this day, on his 60th, it comes out. It slides out of his three-piece waist pocket, moves up a fine curve, the thumb touching the right temple, and halts, thus completing his signature salute. Then, another slow, gentle curve from the brow to the lips, which have, by now, broken into an all-knowing smile.

He blows them kisses with both hands, and they reciprocate with a roar of approval. In the deepest recesses of a democracy's collective mind, a voice persists. Find a superior being. And bow down.

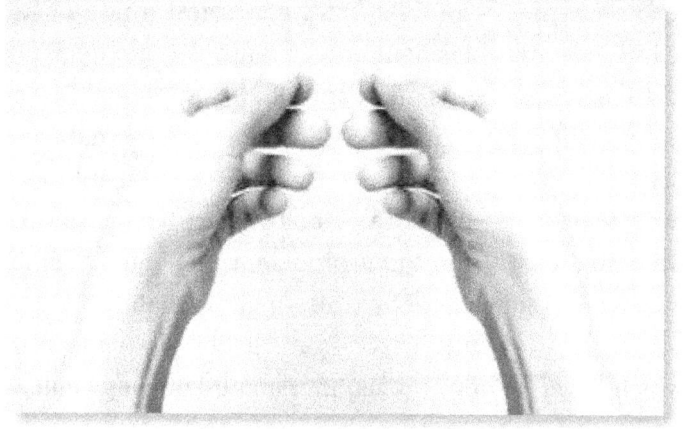

GOALLESS

To not be the man with a purpose, or goal,
a convinced soul his,
Who dare says that we come here, to not play and roll?
A rebel you might be not, but this!?

To do what they did, say what they said,
With sweat and blood paid.
For each slice of laden mirth and glee,
That was supposed to be free!

A paradise lost and regained,
Sans dollars, rubles, yen and rupee,
When I shall love Mary, Kate and Lois nee,
For then, when only humanity remained.

He who lives in perfect ease,
Didn't ever have a boss to appease,

Grateful each night for life, and it's ease.
He with the universal heartbeat that refuses to cease.
He has but one goal – to give,
In the smallest ways each day,
If there ever was a way to go, he knows,
It's this way.

ARTISTE

It's a simple black shirt all the way; unless you choose to look closer, it has a couple of linear frills on the chest, real subtle. It fits, and accentuates the lean cuts on the torso, shoulder tips and the royal V. The difference is, he was a natural, with no gym-toned muscles. He rolled the sleeves, exposing sinister sinews on both lean and strong forearms. There was no watch. Only the ball bearing of a steel ring on his left pinky. The trousers were a nice brick red, and sharp.

And the shoes. They were the most expensive looking fakes you would ever see. Artists know their dress and style, even while they are struggling, before fame arrives. His exposed left foot sock was the only giveaway, with a small skin-exposing, stretched but small, oblong hole. He waits for his third audition today.

CEO

In this great marketplace,
They sell products and services,
Marry values and share space,
The intent is masked, nevertheless.

Then they transform your house,
With policies and clicks of the mouse,
You pay, then they say what's wrong,
With a century of knowledge, and hours long
You no longer call the shots,
As in marriage, a contract ties the knots.

The marketplace has a king,
He was a prince when he sold,
Now they sell, he is but old,
From the corner office, he guides humanity,
Approves like a king, gives a tenth back for his sanity.
He has practiced humility to curb the beast of an ego.
Oh, you have a name for him, the CEO.

PROTECTOR

When a mother chides her little one, does she know that those tiny toes will someday walk, run, fly and grow in a world with borders, bosses, billions?

Guess, they do.

That someday, she, her child will be alone in a crowd of humanity, in a busy airport somewhere on the other side of her mother's world. She will then dip her hand inside her purse, outside the airport, and stop mid-way to remember for a very brief moment.

On that day of nervously waiting for her biggest examination ever, her hand clutching everything, the perfumes, the lipstick, the spill-proof mascara and tissues deep in her black purse – she didn't bring it! Her luckiest, 'favouritest' pen. She doesn't bring the hand out and starts her run. She needs to run down the University stairs, out the huge wrought-iron gates, cross the street, hail a cab.

The exam starts in 15 minutes! And the moment she turns, in her half-run, she sees her protector. "You forgot this in the car..."

Today when the hand comes out of her bag, it has a small note "Passport, flight tickets in the right zip."

ANCIENT LAND AND
THE KING OF PROMISES

The ancient ones wanted change to lead,
Tired of scams, in sports, coal and arms indeed,
With a mandate so strong, and trust so deep,
A lion from the West they said, ain't no sheep!

Beverage of a billion, in tiny cups he sold,
Young, indoctrinated in the family's fold,
Made his mark as a sharp administrator,
They made him a prince, the master orator.

The earth shook, brothers maimed and spilled,
Blood for religion, while the Prince formed his guild,
With able whips and a disabled state,
He inked the writing and their fate.

The orator Prince promised them all,
A billion minions roared, "A savior at last!"
Who spoke so unlike, so unreal the spell he cast,
When the sun went down, the Prince was King, in his
spiteful gall.

Dividing his land with faith lines drawn,
Taxing the taxed, branding his brawn,
Those gold coins are yours no more,
Here, take these coupons instead, my coffers need the gold you bore!

The King's meals happen on air,
The pilots smile, "Sire, you are our staple dare!"
Kings from distant lands huddle to exclaim,
"Is it really us, the talks... or maybe his childhood aim?"

His language for the enemies laced in spite,
Monologues for billions on a Sunday, and a healthy diet,
The King's judgment day cometh, he must start purveying his land,
Shout from ramparts, podiums – retain his throne and the magic wand.

The old farmer makes light of the kingly promises,
Begs, applies, says cheers with pesticides, till life ceases,
His wife shields his children, attests he was no mad!
For a meagre check, a dim, slim future, she ain't anymore
sad.

The billion voices unite, how long shall we be made?
They mill the booths, bring the king back...
Maybe this time, we shall get our promised shade!

THE THREE DRIVERS

It's an endless coastal road, the kind you've seen in them movies. The cool blue sea meets an equally pristine blue sky at a distant indigo horizon. And you are cruising past the squarish rail guards trapping the sea with frolicking humanity, like endless digital screens, in a breezy Boxster.

You are in the backseat with Corporate. The best thing about him is that he has mastered the art of smiling. He flashes customized smiles, often dozens per hour, each unique, spreading across his angular face with rare ease. The second man is a short, stout, unabashed blabbermouth seated with the driver. His round face and beady eyes try hard to flex, keep up with his political lips, mouth. The third, didn't visit the salon in a long, long time. With his beard and hair flowing all over the backrest, Religion is enjoying his drive today.

ON DIVORCE AND SEPARATION

She is all by herself today, miles away,
The daughter out to school, it's a sunny day.
Dusting a lamp shade where he used to stall,
Drawing deep on his cigarette, eyes fixed on the wall.

Three thin slices of afternoon sun escape the curtains and shine,
One on the chipped tile that he fixed so well, and filled the ugly grout line.
The second ray reaches the tray, on the table where they dined,
Morning teas and late night snacks, pray, why does it all rewind?

The third bounces off the glass and shines on an empty picture square,
Once it had two smiling faces, so much in love, and a blue solitaire.
She can hear their chatter right now, subtle yet so much fun
His laughter wafting through the chest drawers, carpets... Even her hair bun!

Her heartbeats, oh they haven't changed since the first
time he held her gaze,
Till now, when her fingers touch their first board game
– a brownish wooden maze.

THE BOSS

The boss has been demonized for no reason at all. It was they who built a sticky wet cement stairway, where the shoes get stuck at each step – not him! The brave take their shoes off only to get stuck at the next step, this time barefoot. Infinite shoes stuck to these vast steps. Up and away from the struggles and moans below, the boss stands – feet planted firmly on the top stair.

His legs are tired, the soles of the feet exposed, blood and years of grime glisten. And then he speaks, "Automation is key…"

MATERIAL

Of all the virtues of modern living, a mind free of bullshit trumps,
With senses five beaten to a pulp, they feel so down in the dumps!
Oh, for the rays of a golden sun, bright greens and moving feet,
The wind across your face so wise, you have chosen defeat.

Vibrations, tunes, alarms and such, gizmos, food and shoes,
Material has consumed your fertile mind, gifting a shorter fuse.
Say no more! And save your ears for the crickets' evening score,
The eyes for a live match, your touch for her and the tongue for everything more.

Where on earth is earth, I ask, for I don't see a soul,
That stretches its senses, open to love, not just to chase a goal?

One day, this too will pass, a new light shall thence shine,
To free you of all the binds that you so gladly made thine.

That light from deep within, will prove to be your guide,
For that forest path so fascinating, like an angel by your side.
When you think what you need to think and do as you wish,
Still keep it all together, like that beast on a flexi-leash.

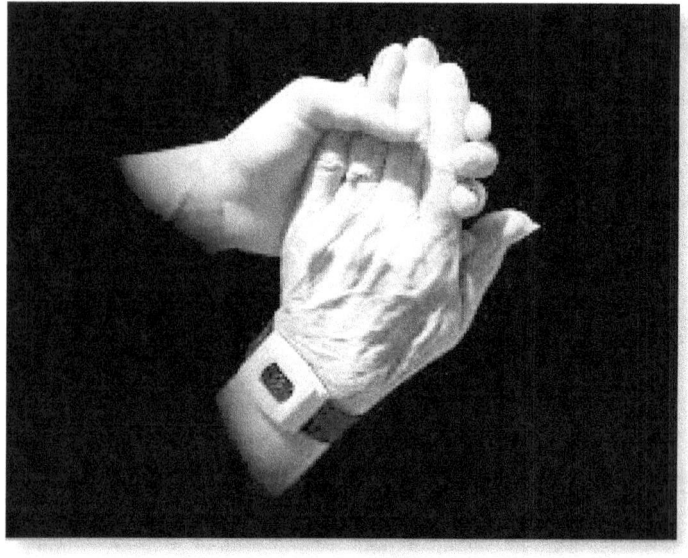

TERMINAL

I realized, lying in my hospital bed, how fragile our life is. While I was cruising on this vast ocean called life, on a lazy Thursday evening, someone tapped me on my shoulder and said, "This is it, your journey was till here."

And I slip gently and dissolve in salt water. All my dreams, all my aspirations brought to this abrupt halt.

It might have slipped from our minds but hear those terminal disease survivors, they all speak alike. It's a great lesson for you and me to just do what we have always known as the right thing. It's a short trip.

HEADS OF STATES

The master of statecraft descends. The moment the gate opens, he is there, black curtains behind – in a white suit with a blue silk pocket square. A triangle of red carpet on an elevated ramp spreads across the airport, flanked with uniformed men standing in attendance. The first bugle sound heralds his first step in the birthplace of organized religion, the land of ambitious empires and a mélange of ethnicities. As he descends, the state head shuffles towards the stairway, an uncontrolled grin on his oblong face.

As the master plants his feet on the ground that had seen religious face-offs for centuries, the head of state embraces him in a tight hug. "This is epic," he says to the master of the largest democracy on the planet, the cradle that embraced his people who fled religious persecution eons ago.

OPINIONATED

The inner truth of what he said, and what she really meant,
Or how the pass should swing by the post, thus a sure opportunity lent,
Or what that minister ought to do, their thoughts like marching minions,
Deep within their deepest minds, create mint fresh opinions.

"The world can live with one less opinion," thus the wise man sayeth.
They said, "Good luck with that, but we shall not betray our faith."
Politics, sports, bosses and religion, humanity, environment and energy,
Thanks to my opinions alone, the world has a sense of synergy!

We opine on women's health and how this world is doomed,
How the World War III is imminent, as long as intents are assumed.
Or how the smartphones now, are ruining the very fabric of life,
And how I used to chop salads, while she sat and sang — my one and only wife.

This mad rush to dump my version, my processed truth on you,
Has to stop for opinions' sake, when yours and mine join,
And truly feel the True.

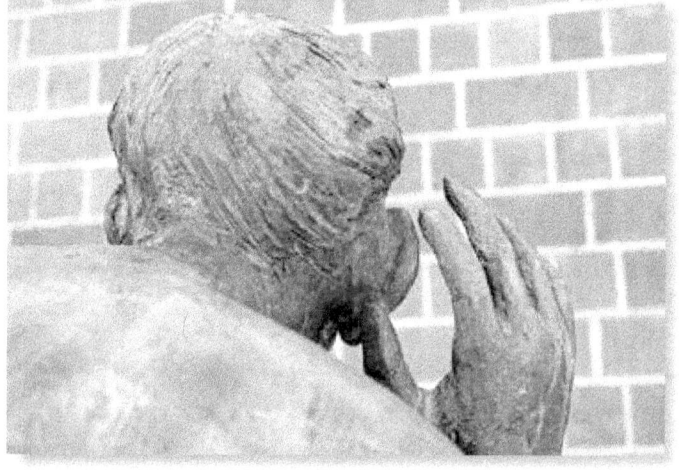

LISTEN

Data is king they say and information, it's processed urban cousin. The modern mind struggles with bills, passwords, names, relationships, clients, dreams, vacations, time, wives, kids, bosses. It is not in the nature of the mind to say no to change. That's a matter of the heart.

So, the mind adapts like those superheroes, ever-adaptive. It breaks up, classifies, decks and stores all the data that the senses soak in, neatly in long corridors of memories with never a whimper. And men take them out at will, put them out to the world like nukes – to incite, coax, sell, sneer, make you laugh, to make you fearful, to spread wisdom. "Listen," He said. Listen!

DÉJÀ VU –

The highway is lined with a coarse brown terrain —
sand, dry shrubs and cacti,
Inside the air-cooled van they sit, swaying with each
turn, drinking black tea.
And then, in a flash he sees her, his woman of many
dreams, sitting alone on a desert rock,
The lump in his throat but a word of four letters —
"Stop!" The driver doesn't take stock.

Once in the hotel, he had this deep belonging – to the
hotel, the sand and the crimson evening,
He takes little rest and then sets out to see that woman
he thought he knew so well, a divine being.
He retraces the same road — back to where he saw her
in passing, heart thumping in his chest,
Reaching the rock where she was seated, he calls out a
name that only he knows best.

From the distant hut she comes out, smiling at him and walking till the sandstone rock,

"Where have we met? And how do you know my name?" she asks, holding the fluttering veil.

Before he starts to answer, his hands cold even in this sweltering heat,

She adds "I have seen you forever in my dreams, come in, let's eat."

DEJA VU

TAROT

"There are new beginnings, which are a result of transformation, a lot of work that has gone in over the past few months. That is when, out of the passion, new flowers are blooming, cutting through all the clouds and bringing a new warmth which you've been longing for." His eyes welled up.

In radiofrequency ablation, a needle is inserted into the center of the lesion and current is applied to generate heat; the tumor cells are killed by cooking. The doctors said it's a miracle. He was no new student to faith.

He watched her 'readings' every day on YouTube and this last one for Virgo, his Zodiac, made it happen. Some call it Tarot, some faith.

AMBITION

For not all toil for a hungered soul,
With satiation recent, of an ancestor's goal,
Then some desires, over many lives snowball,
To wind up a tiny heart, to win hearts, fight battles,
Create, sustain, destroy gently or with gall.

Mom's sweet sunrise words, birds tweet behind,
Ripples and layers of morning sounds,
Filling up the conscious one's very mind,
They remember now, middle and stout,
For this I stretched my wings beyond bounds?

You loved and you lusted, eye on the material,
Like your skin, the heart too peels,
All those experiences, thoughts at which you cringed,
Gave life to a glowing heart, new, though singed.

ODDS

There are Chinese, Koreans, and the locals at this table. The checkered red dots are all over, it's their moment of truth.

"No more bets!"

One of the locals picks the cards with outstretched hands. The moment he holds the three cards, his palms go down, bent like a tent, right thumb facing the left. And then he borrows universal time to go in slow motion. The Chinese draws on his cigarette deeply. The four Korean friends are looking intently at the cards.

Each stack of bet coins are placed neatly on the 'Banker'. Not a single eye caught a big coin pile slide on to the table moments before the call – all coins on 'Player'. He is not your usual tall, dark, and handsome. A medium in all possible measures, except his mind. As he flicked his thumb and index, the cards flew past the board – a natural nine!

The dealers, the slot, and the floor change attendants – all rise around the table, wide-eyed, frozen-faced. But the rest of them – the customers, clap for a full minute for the biggest win they have ever witnessed.

He collects the coins in a black sling, stands up and moves out – gently pushing the burgundy chair back in its place. He had timed it right, once the cashier was done with the last piece of paperwork, the message chimed in his trouser pocket. He had chosen lifetime payment – to pay to the army research hospital miles away from civilization, high in the mountains. The same one that had taken in 52 martyred soldiers a full year back – some alive, some lifeless.

He kept his promise to his dying friend, "Will help set up world-class emergency rooms right here, my friend, I promise – against all odds."

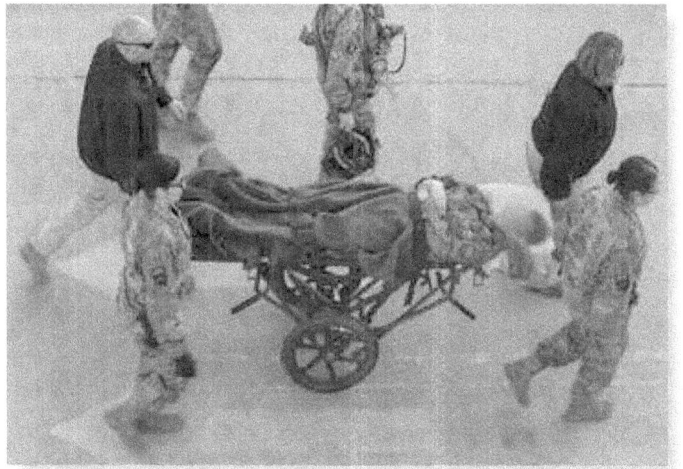

SHEEP

The rebel sheep spoke at last, her bleat strong with purpose,
All the sheep listened deep, this news in sheep-land abuzz.
She spoke of fortitude, legacy and a sense of stewardship,
Adversity, challenges and the need to get a grip.

All sheep cheered, made a promise common yet so somber,
The rebel sheep couldn't help but break a toothy smile asunder.
Network well, meet and greet, and cocktails right after,
Dawn breaks on this vast poolside, burying the last sheep laughter.

When the day of judgment, once so far, felt so damn near,
The sheep were busy rehearsing what the judge needed to hear.
All hail the judge and the sheep! In the stand Ms Rebel,
The hearing starts, halts and rolls like a shingle beach pebble.

The moment of truth is here at last! The sheep to keep
their promise,
Called to the witness stand, one by one, trembling, they
all piss.
The stink makes the jury cringe, the courtroom is all but
calm,
Ms. Rebel's appeal withdrawn, she looks at Mr. Ram.

On their way back home, the wise Ram minces no words
for her,
"You may forgive the sheep in them, but darling, they
will remember."

RETURN OF THE SON

The rumble of the twin engines resonated with the one inside his chest. Only, the one within was deeper, bigger, louder, like a hundred cloud bursts.

"Good Morning! Ladies and Gentlemen. Welcome aboard this flight to La La Land. From Captain Graham and the crew, it is our…"

His eyes were in a trancelike fix on the airline magazine while his hands snapped the buckle in place. He, Mr. Gifted Brouhaha, was returning home after a series of life-altering milestones. The beginning of the end was an ego-induced, Mixed Management Arts display with a boss several rungs senior. Inside, he knew his reputation wasn't relevant anymore; he was breaking free. Next, he said "no more" to his wife of two decades, at the risk of getting his daughter raised with doubtable values. And then he called them.

Two of the most ethereal beauties – bereft of any morality, direction or purpose, ladies of the dark. Both wanted to be Mr. Gifted' s bedmates, but he knew better. They could set any dance, business or banquet floor on fire, all he did was channelize their feminine energies to build businesses of sins. Cigars, Whiskeys and Condoms.

Today, in the plane, with all three businesses sold, he visualizes the world's largest women's university right outside his parents' small town – his hometown. On the back of the airlines magazine, he jots down the subjects –

Anatomy & Physiology
Astronomy
Counselling
Hospitality
Music
Nurturi...?

OF GODMEN AND SPIRITUALITY

The template has been set – a thousand years back,
First create your values core, and then a belief pack.
Next, be generous, and borrow from the greats,
Preach more till you get it right – start with dear mates!

Sanitize your unknown past, for now it shall all be
known,
Just the way you want it to be, don't spare your own!
Friends, and friends of friends, and all the folks who
knew,
Must now sing lofty praise, of your childhood – on
your cue.

The wealthy get drawn to you, so they find a soul,
To tell them all is fine, so what if your wealth is foul?
Make them buy you urban wood, or green farms out of
town,
As long as you bless them right, they shalt bow their
heads way down.

Read up on all that you can – History, Science, and
News,
So when they call you to that Dias grand, serve them
Godly views.
Set aflame social media, get them followers to promote,
For what's a cult that doesn't sing or dance, flatter
neither dote?

When you have done all these and more, you can then
proclaim,
"Leave all your Gods and their Godliness, come play
this simple game!"
Allow me to flood your senses, your mind and your
very soul,
For once I leave, you will see, there was but just a
simple goal.

Every man, is but a child, so lost in this sea,
Anyone that holds his hand, sets his innocence free…

NEO-COLONIST

The Colonist's grandson stands tall in this busy coffee shop that originated in his ancestor's land. His neo-colonial grandfather had promised to help the little brown locals a full century ago, before ruling them.

Today the grandson's entitlement is complete – he orders his drink, eyeing the server's full breasts, a rarity in this part of the world. She is used to this, a sub-conscious acceptance practiced over centuries of occupation. From where he stands, the world is beautiful – a native wife to help him navigate through banking, investments, the household and children. And a plum position in a homeland company with endless benefits to whet yet another family of excesses. "Sir, your double shot is ready for pickup." Smiling across the gay, efficient server, he picks his drink – another bright, expat day.

HUMANITY BORN

Ladies and Gentlemen of the Knowledge Age,
Wear your humanity…
If I could offer you only one advice for the future,
Humanity would be it.

The choices in your life could affect a few or many,
Your best experiences of love, longing, joy, but epiphany
Make your choices from the menu, staid and proven,
But be foretold, it's freedom with matrix handwoven.

So tread, touch, break, join with care,
It's the humane sea, for you to share.
In a world with kindness and gratitude rare,
Where love's a transaction, raw and bare.

Our gifts to the future, should you choose to embrace,
Are humanity and a little grace…
The distilled truth is often revealed,
When you are cocooned and sealed,
In the labyrinth of your mother's womb.

Where the deepest changes in this world happened,
While she ensconced you in the safest haven,
An ocean of information, your ancestry's mess,
Dawned upon your curled consciousness —
The distilled truth flashed, and you were born.

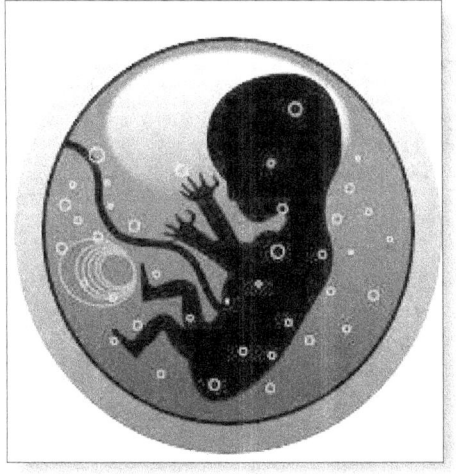

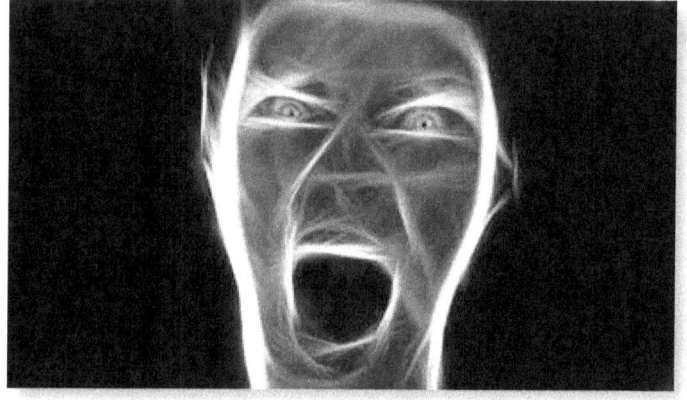

ANGER

For the first time in nine years, she saw it so close – holding it close to her nose this Sunday morning. The smells were unmissable, woody citrus mixed with his fresh coconut. A phallus so refined, yet the veins screamed out at you.

"Is it angry or upset?" she asks sleepily while gently pulling down the soft skin.

"Yes, it's angry," he says. "It's angry for the human insecurities, insensitivities, soft-pedaling of real issues, the lack of integrity in public life, the way entire nations are waking up and guzzling information without filter through the fishing day, the way life goes on even if they know of the certain death of an entire species, the way they ignore – not realizing that life ignores them, the global unrest each day, that terrorism is a part of everyday life, the exes repeating the same mistakes, unemployment of the worthy, heaps of data and shrinking wisdom..."
"Hun?"

Her eyes closed, her mouth is open near his right waist line – she sleeps.

"...and the loss of humanity."

CRESTED IBIS

Gee! I am not the bird that brings home stuff,
Art décor, furniture, books and such fluff!
I made a nest on top of this hill,
Gave you my rare seed, and a bonny Bill.

Now I must fly across the great skies in search,
Of meaning, higher purpose, and food for thought,
For what's a bird that hasn't spread its majestic wings,
Flown over lands and oceans, befriending commoners
and kings?

Wait for me if you must, for when I return,
I shall have gifts as no lady could spurn.
Wisdom, experience and an imperceptible sense of
humor,
Your young lover in a mature plume, a wiser late-bloomer.

GUINNESS

He locked down on two final probable records, both honed during his 6 years in military – the first was ear wiggling, and the second, spinning a dining plate endlessly on any of his left hand fingers.

"Dear Maxine,

We are pleased to inform you that your record application for Highest number of ear wiggles in a minute has been received and you do not need to do anything further at this stage." He held the device to his chest and dreamt that night.

His little girl running towards him on a misty green valley – "Papa you are a record breaker!" The next day he sent the wife the draft separation papers.

FAMILY

They have all come together to mourn one of their own,
The one they despised the most, and disdain shown.
Mourning turns to celebration, just to make things light,
The rainforest comes alive, birds chirp, hoot, tweet, take
flight.

One of the brothers sits out of the tents, soaked in the
tropical rain,
He examines a leaf, a dozen thoughts in his brain.
The eldest comes out, sits behind and asks,
"What keeps my brother up, the man of many masks?"

The younger passes the leaf and says, "This is our
family leaf…
The mid vein our surname, and all the secondaries are
us,
Now that she is gone, the leaf is torn right here, thus.

CRAWLERS AND THE BLUE HORIZON

Like the minions in a mobile game, the crawlers crawled forward – millions of them! One of the crawlers in the left flank stopped. He looked around to see his sisters, brothers, colleagues and known faces. And then he looked forward towards the finish line. He whipped out his latest gadget from the left pocket and typed furiously into it, even with the crowd pushing him to move.

The result was scary!

He needed exactly 17 years, 4 months and 23 days to reach the Finish Line. He turned back, ambling past the huge surging crowd on the left flank, he started a slow run. The left and right flanks had 'borders' almost two meters high, made up of earth, rubble, pebbles and such. As he began to run, his lungs started to energize his lean body like never before. His heart rate picked up a steady beat in seconds, and he ran like the wind! As he reached top speed, the left flank of the crawling minions suddenly opened up to a vast open land with a blue horizon and he could now see the sea from where he was! Soon he perceived his misjudgment—between his higher ground and the sea-like horizon was an undulating land mass of thick forests, albeit at a lower altitude. He didn't stop his run. He ate wild berries, bruised himself, found fresh water deep in the woods, half slept, but continued his run.

Almost a full 2 years later, he was out of the woods – craggy and bearded but still running, with his eyes set on the blue horizon. Now he could see the waters clearly and then he saw them.

An unending land with sea beaches with multi-colored earth dwellings, shades, and tents spread till the eyes can see. A busy commune of divergent crawlers – busy with all kinds of work. They were building a new civilization out here. Everything was natural, each material earthy, and the people – well, everybody moved with purpose, and a dignity that was natural. Each at her or his highest human evolution.

He had arrived – 15 years, 4 months and 22 days early.

LIMITLESS LTD.

You have but a limited number of breaths, spouses, laughs,
Orgasms, heartbreaks, meals, tears, weddings and photographs.
Deep in the mother's womb, each of these designed, predefined,
You and your excesses won't alter the sum of a life so refined.

You might think of that one more breath after your last,
And a trophy spouse to add to your repertoire vast,
Each time you go against the grain, the design resets,
Only for the twigs in the stream, true fulfilment begets.

And then there is love, gratitude and kindness rare,
Humanity's noblest virtues, all limitless, but you unaware
Chasing the limited, tangible, the material,
So many through the ages have ignored this..
For a decorated, yet unfulfilled soul's burial.

Give till it hurts, and be grateful, for it might have not,
To be limited in what you expect, yet limitless in thought.

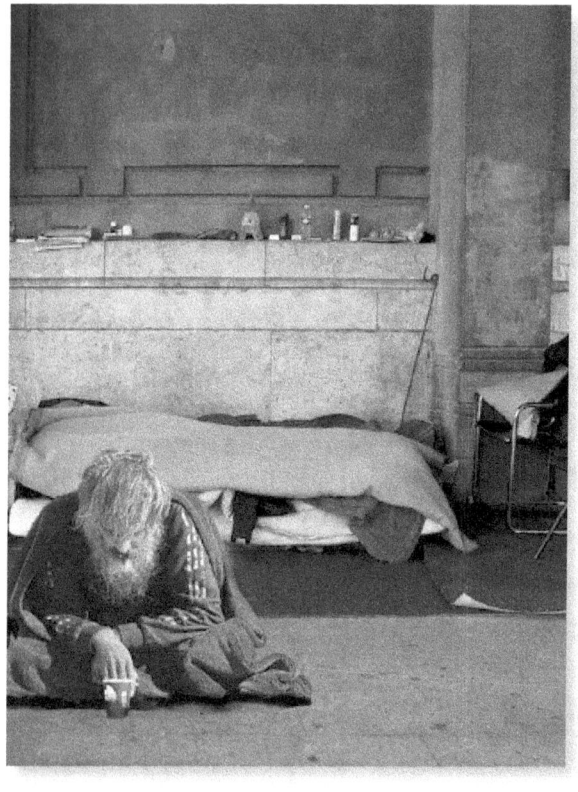

BEAUTIFUL PLANET

The tramp is punctual. Before the last city lights go off, and the first hopes of a day are born, he wakes up. His craggy, broad face looks up at the sky, eyes shut tight, spine erect. He says a silent prayer. He has been balding in patches, the silvery brown hair that fall over his ears, neck and shoulders, are somewhat matted. His shaky, hairy right hand pushes down the blanket upon which he is seated, hoisting the rest of his body up. His limp left leg is an embarrassment that he tries to cover up by moving his upper body more while walking.

He pays the exact change to the short, pudgy man at the public comfort room counter, goes in and gets out in under 15 minutes. The ritual is the exact same each day – shake out the blanket of any dust, keep his 'world' neatly stacked along the wall behind, and then sit with an erect spine for the following 4 'office hours'. Back resting against the 5-star hotel wall, a cushion in between – the guards let him be, after years of humiliation and his silent persuasion.

He keeps his aluminum bowl and steel container without the lid in front, collects himself and then puts 'them' on.

His black shades – if you look closely at the tinted glass, you would see the first lights of dawn upon a beautiful planet.

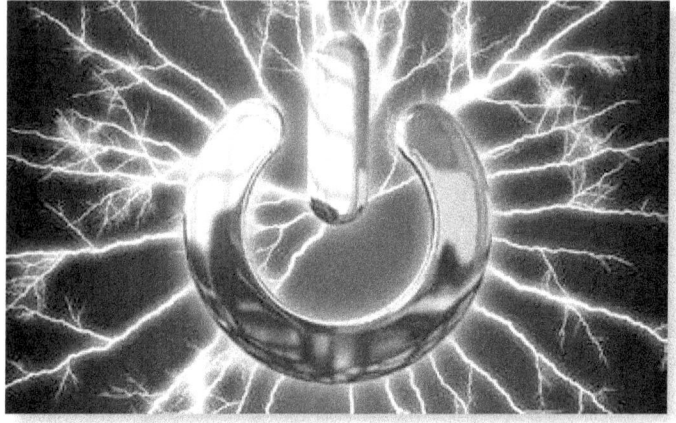

POWER

Once upon a time, your muscles defined power,
Then came the plants and machines, and then the
cellphone tower.
Now, in the age of information, your muscles don't mean
a thing,
The farmers now tend data farms, for data is the new
king.

If you know a thing about others, you can sure leverage,
Think of knowing nations together, privacy no more a
privilege.
So the powerful now are the ones that know both you
and me,
More than our deepest friends, and they admit that with
glee!

Knowing my secrets makes you powerful, so be it, my
social friend,
May my powers be joined with you, till the very end.
For the real power is in joining ranks, dreams and shared
vision,
Heed this, not a preach, the world needs our unison.

ROMANTIQUE

Lilac cushions, caramel and blue linen, blue and white drapes matching the handwoven floor rug. The petals are hidden under the comforter. She chose gold and whites at the dining area with the silver horse snout brushing against the wines in the bucket. A dozen flickering candles spread across the hallway, bath and bed – each witness to the meticulous florals on their mistress's glistening nail paint. Now-a-days, it was a phone message, never the doorbell.

She opens the door to a light evening rain, shining roads, and him. For the first time in their 23 years of doorway greetings, they didn't close the door. Standing in silence in the doorway, the kiss lasts just under a minute. She takes him by one hand, his coat in the other, and walks – this walk he knows only too well. He lifts her with that gentle upswing, right after they enter the bedroom, both eyes riveted on her lashes. Her body arches up at her bosom, making a curve that stretches right down to where he holds her with his naturally broad, right forearm.

Seating his queen down gently on his king-size platform bed, he puts on the music they first danced to. The soft breeze creates ripples in the caramel curtains, matching flickering candle flames swaying to their every move. John Legend comes alive in this room, two reunited souls tucked away in a faraway chalet.

POISON IVY

You are brought up to be mannered, yet bred for the kill,
Never too protected, barring mama's waffles and grill.
Horses, tennis and violin by six, athletics, piano too in
the mix,
Regimented, disciplined – like that old song on bricks.

They soon call your sarcasm, and your attitude cavalier,
You never cared… Oh the drugs – they have no fear.
The schools are few, the dreamers many,
Your first day at Ivy but an epiphany.

Small dorm rooms, dining hall food,
Track and field, campus girls in hood.
You had your fill early, though not wise,
Found divinity, in the devil's disguise.

You start work, with the famous six figure,
Eighteen hours, luncheons and dreams bigger.
On your thirtieth, passed out in a drunken bout,
Trembling on the high rise ledge, a classic burnout.

The Ivy is clingy, yet symbol of eternal life,
Your life's worth is much more — than a career and strife.

DEATH OF AN ACT

The wisp of a silent smoke, bluish white but unerringly straight, rises from a ceramic hotel ashtray. The cigarette is burnt till about a fifth from the base of the white filter.

The ash is such an artful heap; suddenly, the smoke flickers with a simultaneous rustle of the bathtub curtain. The actress' last breaths are deep, halting and laborious, as if something is clogging her airways.

Her left hand fails at trying to clutch the wet curtains, while the legs, weak with exhaustion, bend one last time and come to a standstill. She was enacting death a while ago, nostrils pinched by the left forefinger and thumb, body and face underwater and in seconds, as if in a whirlpool, her mind projects swirling images, rotating anti-clockwise at higher than life speed.

Of her best cinematic moments – jumping across buildings, dancing with abandon, smiling her signature highbrow smile, singing under the rain, screaming at the villain, kissing her onscreen lover's cheeks, crying helplessly over her father's still body, swimming across the pool in her favorite orange two-piece... and the sabbatical. They said it was an overdose, she smiles – just her final act.

The wisp of bluish white smoke dies out on its own.

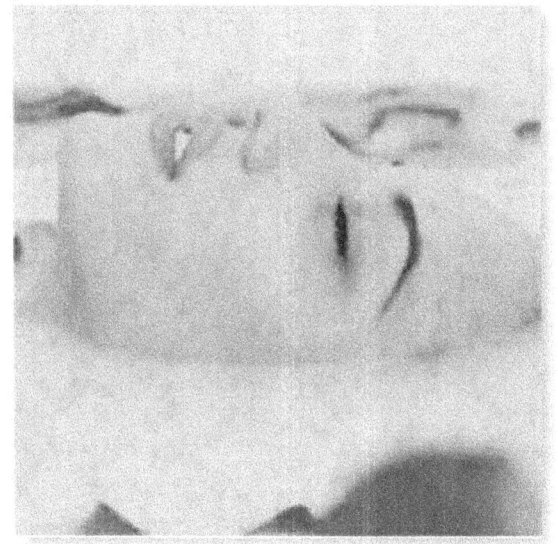

LONG FACES

Look at your long face – you entitled rich kid, daddy's boy!
Has he not given you all you wished for and so much joy?
Took you to the glitzy tables, the bland board rooms, and why?
So you sit and sulk on that couch, drugged and so ready to fly?

I see you at the bar, so full of shrugs, borrowed pride and a long face,
As if a great responsibility to redeem rests on you someplace...
Ah, it's your tender shoulders, boy will you be able to redeem?
Cause you are busy killing on screen, while daddy smiles in his dream.

We are fine with all of that, if each cent was yours,
An able mind with the means to provide food, shelter
and cures.
Why not further what the old man giveth and use your
life so vast?
We would like more of you in the quest to make this
planet last.

You would be smiling then, having found yourself,
The shadow of your beautiful face on that torn migrant
elf.

INTERVIEW INCARNATE

"Hey, Good afternoon!"

"Good afternoon."

"Please have a seat. So you are David Reinhardt, did I get it right?"

"You got it."

"I was watching your video just before you came in. Splendid job!"

"Thanks, you are generous. Must admit, it was fulfilling."

"So, did you get a chance to go through the..."

"Yes, I did. We got to niggle and wiggle a bit on the appendices... we will do just fine."

"Okay then, can I detail this out to you on screen?"

"Please, by all means..."

"Alright, here we go. This is what a "grid" will look like. Any matter within the grid will be self-propelled. No transmission losses and minimal infrastructure costs. The first two grids are operating in these parallels here… and here. Any ideas at this point?"

"Later."

"Right. And the third is being built right here, about 20 kms inland. We wanted to know if you could take over all three sites. Also, if you would be able to divide time between the three. No virtual scheisse. Come, let me show you the bird's-eye view of the project."

As the two men walk on the high-gloss, beige stone floor, the corridor opens up to a tempered glass deck on the east wall of a stiff mountain. The view outside is that of a misty morning, the highway below, a tiny grey, winding ribbon. The interviewer's shoe squeaks and clunks throughout, on the polished floor. At about halfway, he halts and looks down at the interviewee's shoes. And then slowly looks up at his deep-set, slanted eyes.

"Rubber soles? Hey!" In a split second it dawns upon him, he was looking 'up' at a man a full 1.5 inches shorter a while ago in the interview room.

The interviewee was a couple of inches above the floor – floating.

"You didn't watch the full video. I am the 4th grid."

THE FEARLESS BADGER

The badger in you must first shake off your fear,
Then wake up and get your gear,
A surgeon, a teacher, a workman you may be,
Each morning, the goal is abundantly clear.

You smile at the naggers and resolve not to judge,
Each bigger problem but a blessing, not a smudge.
Silently fearless, you march on,
Your shield is your humility and your sword, your skillset
drawn.

No one ever has or ever will question,
The possibilities of the fearless one.

LATE GRAMMY

The late bloomer is all of 43 today. His societal diktat states that one should be at their peak, be nicely settled and gather everything they can by 32-34. Well, he averaged all the suggestions, and today he is 11 years 3 months behind! The spotlight turns a crystal like bluish white, the hosts look up at the AV, and the announcer says it, "For best compilation soundtrack album, the nominees are..."

He had practiced this walk in his hotel suite the night before and many nights before yesterday, on the cow-skin lookalike carpet at home. Walk fast with the drums, lightly touch the tip of your nose with the base of your left thumb, fingers half bent, pointing up. Running up the stairs, practiced on the couch at home and the settee at the hotel, in sync with the lounge beat drums.

Bend forward, receive the award and thank three people. All three family members. It's organic – for the first time, starting with the front row, the entire 8000 rise to clap. The best music to his abused ears.

MUSIC FORGOTTEN

A Musician, Singer and Songwriter of yesteryears,
This educated, erudite man of many spheres.
Guitar in hand and his trademark bandana,
Had the world at his feet, with his dangling Havana.

Mellifluous, charming, sexy, they said,
Of his voice and his music so ahead...
Of times and the world, he never missed a chance,
To woo the ladies with his on-stage dance.

An addiction and several wives later,
Worldwide concerts, composing music greater!
Yesterday I saw him on television,
Suddenly so old, maybe a sentient decision.

The eyes so deep, wavy silver hair and a colored headband,
The guitar still in his wrinkled hands, behind him the desert sand.
"Music is a service of love, it's a language that doesn't require a syllable."
He thus speaks looking away from the camera, his deep melancholy palpable.

Surrounded by his last few followers, in a desert adobe smoking dope,
Forgotten by this world, he sings a new song... one of enduring hope.

CORPORATE NOOSE

You might not say it, but the men have a short hair template, hence the uniformity. Ditto for the ladies – there is an unseen diktat for the length, color, and an unexplained silken straightness. Their dress choices too are borne out of some unseen, unwritten commandment, hence uniform.

When they stand in a queue for the elevators, while waiting for their orders at the cafe, while smoking, while waiting for their turn at the comfort rooms, or doing nothing, they are looking at screens of all sizes, sucked into a wonder-world of text and pictures.

And each one of them have it around their necks – a beaded steel string, a polyester ribbon, or a braided paracord with a card in a card holder. While they are aware of their shirts and suits, and boots and belts, they forget this important noose around their necks, their visa to a vast cosmos of hierarchies, clients, appraisals, and processed, dry creative juices.

The noose is lifelong. Welcome to the corporate.

OLDER

And I shut out all the noise to keep my sanity and brilliance,
How else could I accept that Mhyra, Joy and Ally would no more dance?
We danced the slow-mo dance, in college, office and the retiree's ball,
I still see Mhyra's index finger move hair away from a radiant face and stall.

And then beckon us three to the limelight – Ally the first to go,
They played Latin beats, Ally and her four legged crutch, oh what a show!
Joy was the far corner dancer, with just one hand in the air,
Like an orchestra conductor, we loved his old style and flair.

And I was in the center, cheering, jeering, the clown in
the mix,
Four friends forever, in our golden years, yet so full of
tricks!
Berlin, Ibiza, Kiev, Rome and Helsinki, we have toured,
Danced with our pains and all our old age woes, cured.

Alas, earlier today, our WhatsApp group has only me
alive to dance.
I shut out all the noise, to keep my sanity and brilliance.

BLUE MOON

The white blinds were up at his chest level– a fedora, a bow tie, and a brief adorned an ex-rugged, now smooth body. She was behind him, matching his steps – a perfect foil. While they danced away on a rare blue moon night, the rest of the world slept. She was the DJ tonight – all her best dance songs come alive in his 'castle'.

His credentials were not much. It was only this, he was at each music event worth the time, across continents, straddling all genres. And she was his itinerary creator and dance partner.

DATING IN THE DARK

He says a silent 'sorry' with each smooth left swipe,
Alas Hun, you seem nice and fun, but really not my
type!
Though he swipes slow to see each face pass one last
time,
A bunch of bright and could-be dreams swept off in
early prime!

"If you don't understand my silence, you won't know
my words,"
And many such deep down quotes, make men out of
real nerds.
Or the simpler, "Never let a fool kiss you, or a kiss fool
you" kinds,
Makes them think, "Oh what a thought, can she read
our minds?"

And "Looking for someone who can deal with a new age, female Einstein."
Makes the guys go, "Sure, but why? Thanks, but I'm really fine!"
Endless swipes driven by human longing and lust,
In the end, a short, long or nightly bond the only must.

Gone are those days of silent meals looking deep into each other's eyes,
Smiling, soaking in electric romance, waiting for burgers and fries.

MONK IN THE CITY

The last of the condominium lights go off at 27 minutes past 3. The traffic has died down long back, the crickets are humming a Tuesday tune, there is a hint of moon lighting up the lazy clouds up there. He is busy watching himself, eyelids shut tight, eyeballs still, looking upwards and crisscrossing each other's imaginary dark rays.

The spine is comfortably erect, and the music – an ancient rhythmic beat. The room is pitch dark with only a sliver of yellow light escaping from an upturned magazine on the mouth of a really dim lampshade. He starts moving, a trance-like dance with the slowest of moves. He redefines frugal – two meals a day, minimal social contact, long hours at work and longer hours just seated on his orange mat.

If you care to look closely, the ears twitch, and the naked, naturally-toned body goes into a slow seated dance, perfectly synced with the music. And then it happens. The bolt flashes across the skies, the thunder of a thousand clouds rumbling, and the island's clouds give way to rapturous rains. A monk in the city.

JUICE

Your juice and mine are not the same, yet our faces shine,
You live the prescribed life and walked the trodden path,
While I traverse the world so wide, with nary a silken
bath.

And then that day when we are done, weary and
wizened coarse,
Our wrinkled faces under a heavenly sun, neither joy nor
remorse,
"Was it worth all the fun?" I smile while I say,
"Well one an ass and the other a prick, choose if you
may."

MOUNTAIN SHOES

Both orange, blue and black soles have sticky crystallized mud at the back, the kind that you gather on a semi-dried, sticky mud trail. The fronts have the same – till the point where the soles turn up and meet the base of the heat-resistant synthetic fiber and assorted fabric upper. The neat, long front zip with a blue rubber slider, the orange tongue, black fasteners and the silver shoe within the shoe – he had big feet, a notch over 30 cms.

In about five minutes from now, they are going to start packing everything in this east-end study along with the shoes in neatly-taped brown cardboard boxes.

"So, it's time to go!" Right says to Left.
"Yup, it's time," says Left.
"Remember Serengeti?"
"Why don't you talk about the times and I listen. Never know... maybe they will pack us in separate boxes later."
"Hahaha... man... the first time we set foot on endless grass. And you could see Mount Kilimanjaro in the horizon, the seriousness with which it rose, the flat top.

He always used to move his right toe up and down, stretching my upper and the throat. It meant we had arrived. We took 7 days to climb atop – the chocolatey brown and white snow, the long shadows and the wooden boards of the summit. And then the Alpine Mont Blanc! How white the snow, the three pure white peaks and the deadly silence! But my favorite till date would be Ama Dablam. The hanging glacier, the majestic peak like the head of an eagle and the two peaks on its side, like wings, just about to take flight. I still remember how he lifted me and the foot, angled my back towards you and tapped your back several times."

"Accomplishment."

THE PROFESSIONALS ON POLITICS

The room's highlights are its cobalt and white intricately patterned wallpaper, the in-room Jacuzzi with crystal fittings and the customized Super King bed. The wallpaper pattern extends to the cushions and the bed linen. Two young women seated by the window chairs draw on medium-sized joints without the back. The evening lounge music is this brothel's signature, home-compiled deep house.

"...Never looked at it that way," the first one continues. "We are literally fucked. The government has decriminalized the trade, made it legal and regulated here. However, our taxes have gone up and the demand is lower than before."

"Yep," says the second. "And that is why we need to innovate. Create your own page, tweet your stuff, try website ads. Don't rely on the A-hole." With another deep draw, she passes the joint. She continues "My government hasn't legalized it yet. It's a joke because my President had me and one of my sisters a couple of years back. Such a limp... and a pimp!"

Both break out in hysterical fits. Collecting herself, the first escort lights up, this time a cigarette. "I just hope all of us, all of us girls from twelve nations save up enough for the lifestyle we dream of…once out of this. Gonna see my daughter after 3 months."

"Housekeeping! Ma'am… client is waiting, need to clean up, kindly step out."

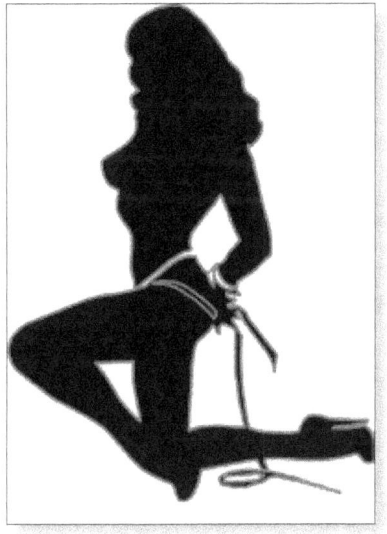

AIRMOS

The airport is a cosmos – each automated motion akin to a star's revolution. Everybody seeking a destination that takes them near or far. The sheer joy of watching the elderly put on their glasses, taking out a piece of paper from the belt pouch and pouring their eyes out on the ticket. The first-time travelers and children, trying to soak in all the sights, sounds and movements. The melting of mechanical and human noise, the announcements and... us.

An unstructured rhythm of human emotions, fallacies and virtues – starting with waves of hands and tears, between the cosmos and the world outside, to rising together during boarding announcements, or to giving way for the window-seat traveler in the cabin, humanity shines.

And the carriers of life, the crafts of superior engineering they stand, taxi, land and take-off – the planets. And all of them walking, talking on the phone, chatting by the bar, buying beers with a slouch and with their hands on the luggage, are the stars – humans.

DIGITAL

You have transcended the meager skills of lighting a fire, making pointed weapons, ploughing, placing and taking off products from the belt, flying a powered craft, and computing. Now you are communicating. Your entire ancestry didn't write as much as you have, the only pictures they posted were on corridor walls, house corners and such. Taking your own picture was both art and vanity. And no one had an unwritten social diktat back then – to 'Like' them.

Banter, goal-agnostic conversations and beautiful silences have been long replaced by virtual fulfillment of another kind. Wait. And this too shall pass, as we grapple with ways to satiate the soul.

FROM HIM TO HER

He was 43, she 12.

"Be true to your intent, don't brood over what's done, be guided by your soul. Choose these 3 wisely – your means to earn, your mentor and friends, and your words. You will have countless chances to reshape what you call life, and only one to live.

Don't choose to sulk, ever, it's not worth it. Learn to keep your thoughts to yourself in work and business, share them amongst friends and family, speak what you must to the commune and put them on paper for your progeny. Since you will live once, do all that your soul silently tells you on countless mornings, sunny and bright."

THE REVENGE AT BALI

The son listens intently to a lamenting dad. "They wrote an article on me, it said "His graceful driving and easy footwork marked him out as a future batsman, and he became one, only to disappoint his admirers." Is this fair? When you perform at the highest levels in sport, and illnesses tear your body apart... Don't they remember the sportsman's agony and talent anymore?"

When the bombs rip apart three blocks along with the nightclub, his son and his wife were in the hotel; the glass windows shattered, glass pieces all over the carpet. "Careful!" said the wife. While his first instinct was to duck and call his friends, he held on to the phone while he ran across the suite and opened the door. Running down and out on the road, he sees countless young, bleeding adults running in all directions. He collects himself, runs to the back of the hotel, past the reception. No one stops him today, in he goes, past the Receivables, Accounts, down the stairs to the Maintenance room. Reaching the lockers, his war cry booms across the corridors, "Get out and give me a hand!" He and his wife, alongwith the hotel staff, triaged victims in the hotel lobby to save hundreds.

When the last burnt woman goes to sleep, it's early daybreak. Ambling past the restaurant, he goes out to this small, lush green outdoor smoking nook. As he lights up, the dad's voice wafts through the smoke, "Well done, Son..."

CREATURES OF THE POSSIBLE

Urban landscapes by night, across the planet, are the same. Headlights and taillights glistening on city roads, soft window lights glowing in the distance in towers of sleeping, frolicking, breeding, reading, bathing, chatting, watching populace.

Down there in the cars, a million moving thoughts on wheels – planning, scheming, watching the tail lights in front, talking to loved ones, and dreaming. Cities by night are creatures of possibilities, ones that spawn ideas for tomorrow. The time when friendly chatter wafts across bars, merges with drums, piano notes and gossip.

OF THINGS TO COME

Villages and provinces moving to the cities, cities converging in metropolises, metropolises merge into megalopolises and the megapolises burst into cosmopolises.

Humanity without borders, guaranteed lifetime freedom, access to life-enhancing injectables and the means to thrive to their highest potential aided by some of the brightest minds.

Women and children have voluntary access to arts of all kinds, the elderly have unique access street booths to record their commentaries on society, the women have the highest freedom in society, from choosing a spouse, to adopting a child, to being openly gay.

Everybody that moves on these streets has a purpose, not for the sake of having a purpose but are driven by it from deep within. Everybody can self-transport within a guided matrix within the cosmopolis, oh and there is no currency anymore, each contribution to the society gives you currency credited to your body chip.